MASTER MORPHOLOGY SKILLS

AGAINST THE ODDS

POMPEII

ELEANOR CARDELL
ILLUSTRATED BY ROBERT BALL

Produced for DK by
Book Buddy Media

Project Editor Amanda Eisenthal
Editor Bryony Brain
Art Editor Anna Scully
Managing Editor Carine Tracanelli
Managing Art Editor Sarah Corcoran
Production Editor Andy Hilliard
Production Controller Rebecca Parton
Publisher Sarah Forbes
Managing Director, Learning Hilary Fine

First American Edition, 2025
Published in the United States by DK Publishing,
a division of Penguin Random House LLC
1745 Broadway, 20th Floor, New York, NY 10019

Copyright © 2025 Dorling Kindersley Limited
25 26 27 28 29 10 9 8 7 6 5 4 3 2 1
001–345263–Jul/2025

All rights reserved.
Without limiting the rights under the copyright reserved above, no part of this publication may be reproduced, stored in or introduced into a retrieval system, or transmitted, in any form, or by any means (electronic, mechanical, photocopying, recording, or otherwise), without the prior written permission of the copyright owner.
DK values and supports copyright. Thank you for respecting intellectual property laws by not reproducing, scanning or distributing any part of this publication by any means without permission. By purchasing an authorised edition, you are supporting writers and artists and enabling DK to continue to publish books that inform and inspire readers.
No part of this publication may be used or reproduced in any manner for the purpose of training artificial intelligence technologies or systems. In accordance with Article 4(3) of the DSM Directive 2019/790, DK expressly reserves this work from the text and data mining exception.

Published in Great Britain by Dorling Kindersley Limited

HC ISBN: 978-0-5939-6270-1
PB ISBN: 978-0-5939-6269-5

DK books are available at special discounts when purchased in bulk for sales promotions, premiums, fund-raising, or educational use.
For details, contact: DK Publishing Special Markets,
1745 Broadway, 20th Floor, New York, NY 10019
SpecialSales@dk.com

Printed and bound in the UK

www.dk.com

This book was made with Forest Stewardship Council™ certified paper – one small step in DK's commitment to a sustainable future. Learn more at **www.dk.com/uk/information/sustainability**

CONTENTS

MASTERING MORPHOLOGY 4
VOCABULARY LIST 6
CHAPTER 1 9
CHAPTER 2 17
CHAPTER 3 26
CHAPTER 4 34
CHAPTER 5 43
CHAPTER 6 51
CHAPTER 7 58
CHAPTER 8 67
CHAPTER 9 76
CHAPTER 10 84
CHAPTER 11 94
CHAPTER 12 102
CHAPTER 13 110
CHAPTER 14 118
CHAPTER 15 128
DISCUSSION QUESTIONS 138
THE TRUTH BEHIND THE TALE 140

Mastering Morphology

What is Morphology?

Morphology is the study of the structure of words. Breaking new words down into smaller parts can help you to understand the word's meaning.

As you read more words with the same small parts, you will start to decode and understand these words more quickly. This builds fluency and comprehension which helps us become lifelong readers!

What Are Base and Root Words?

Base words like *play* can stand alone.

Root words like *-loc* need a prefix or suffix and cannot stand alone. We can add prefixes and suffixes to base and root words to change their meaning.

Can you **replay** that song?

I am a soccer **player**.

The family decided to **relocate**.

What Are Prefixes and Suffixes?

Prefixes are word parts added to the beginning of words to change their meaning.

un + happy → unhappy (not happy)

mid + night → midnight (middle of the night)

Suffixes are word parts added to the end of words. Suffixes can change a word's meaning in multiple ways.

joy + ful → joyful (full of joy)

rain + ed → rained (the rain already happened)

dog + s → dogs (more than one dog)

Using Word Parts to Read New Words

In this book, you will see many words with common noun suffixes. To decode a word like this, break the word into its base and suffix. Determine the meaning of each of these word parts and put the meanings together.

hard + ship → hardship

arrive + al → arrival

bright + ness → brightness

Vocabulary List

In this book, you will read many words with common noun suffixes. The suffixes you will read are listed below.

-s, -es, -ment, -ness, -er, -ship, -hood, -ist, -or, -al, -tion, -sion

Here are some of the words you will read in this book.

arrival (noun): the act of showing up somewhere
arrive + al

SPELLING RULE: when adding a suffix that begins with a vowel to a base or root word that ends in *e*, *e* is dropped and replaced by the suffix

businesses (noun): more than one business or company
busi + ness + es

companionship (noun): the feeling and enjoyment of spending time with other people
com + pan + ion + ship

division (noun): the act of something separating
divi + sion

eagerness (noun): a strong and impatient feeling
eager + ness

gladiator (noun): a person who fights in arenas to entertain an audience
gladiat + or

government (noun): the system of rules and the people who make and administer them
govern + ment

helper (noun): a person who provides assistance
help + er

livelihood (noun): the way in which someone earns money to support themselves
live + ly + hood

SPELLING RULE: the *y* in the suffix *-ly* changes to *i* when an additional suffix is added

merchants (noun): people who buy, sell, and trade goods
merchant + s

mosaicist (noun): a person who makes mosaics or tiles
mosaic + ist

CHAPTER 1

Fabia closes her eyes and takes a deep breath. She imagines the street in front of her and the stepping stones in the middle that most people use to cross. She doesn't need them, though. This is the day. Today, she'll finally attempt the jump all the way across to the sidewalk on the other side.

The sounds around her fade away. All that's left is her focus, her certainty. She's going to make it. Fabia lets out her breath, opens her eyes, and jumps. The whole time she's in the air, she keeps her eyes on her landing spot getting closer…closer…

Her feet land short, her toes clinging to the sidewalk while her heels hang over the street.

Her arms flail and she tries to lean forward even as she feels herself tipping back.

"Fabia!" A hand grabs her, yanking her forward and onto the sidewalk. She stumbles. Her heart races as she finds her footing on the pavement.

"Thanks, Titus," she says, looking over at her twin brother. He leans heavily on his crutch with a look of exasperation.

"Someday, you're going to fall, and I won't be around to catch you," he says.

Fabia glances back across the narrow street. She'd made the jump from the crossing stones in the middle before. Leaping all the way across is the next logical step. "I think it was pretty good for a first try."

"I still don't understand *why* you want to jump all the way over."

"It's fun! Also, what if I want to cross and it's a long way to the nearest crossing? I should be able to jump." Fabia looks past the stones to the street itself. "I don't want to step in...that." A brown sludge runs along the lower part of the street, settling into the cart tracks and overfilling them. Fabia doesn't even want to know what's in it.

"Just go down to the crossing like everyone else," Titus says, starting off down the sidewalk. His bag bumps against his hip with every uneven step. "Come on, Fabia. I don't want to be late for class."

Fabia takes off after him, checking quickly to see that the coins her mother had given her are still wrapped in the cloth at the bottom of her basket. Fabia would get in a lot of trouble if she accidentally lost the day's bread money in her eagerness to jump over the street.

Her neighborhood is already full of action. Stores and workshops are opening their doors to the street as people begin their days. Merchants are setting out wares and advertising their services. The sharp smell of fish sauce wafts out of one storefront.

Fabia takes a deep breath as she passes by, enjoying the smell of the city. She dodges a dog lying panting on the sidewalk and continues weaving around shopkeepers and artisans. She avoids running into anybody as she follows Titus down the street.

"There's no need to hurry so much," Fabia says when she catches up. "You're not going to be late."

Still, when they come to the next crossing, Fabia takes the stepping stones right behind her brother. She knows how important it is for him to get to class on time.

Titus pauses on the other side, waiting for her arrival.

"You know, you don't need to walk with me to school every day. I know how to get there myself," says Titus.

"But I like it! We get to hang out, and I get out of the house."

Fabia always enjoys Titus's companionship. She worries about him, too, though she'd never admit it to him.

He gets along well on his crutch, but Fabia knows that people don't always pay attention, and it would be easy to knock him over without even noticing. Titus wasn't big before his accident, and he hasn't grown that much since.

After walking a few more minutes, they emerge from the shadowed city street into the dazzling white stone of the Forum.

The Forum is an enormous square, full of statues of the emperors of the past and lined with large, imposing buildings.

On one end is the Temple of the Triad, dedicated to the gods Jupiter, Juno, and Minerva. It sits high at the top of a set of stairs, with columns reaching toward the sky.

It had been damaged in an earthquake many years before and is still awaiting restoration.

Even as it is, the structure is impressive. It commands the attention of anybody crossing the Forum. Mount Vesuvius rises behind it, its sides sloping up smoothly toward the peak.

Fabia pauses for just a moment like she does every morning, looking up at the mountain.

In the fresh, bright light of the new day, it's easy to imagine that the gods worshipped in the temples might live at the top, watching over the city of Pompeii.

CHAPTER 2

Fabia turns away from the mountain and looks out over the Forum.

Across from them at the other end are the government buildings. She can already feel the liveliness of the Forum this morning.

Men in togas bustle in and out, some of them carrying official-looking documents.

Fabia and Titus make sure to stay out of their way. Priests and priestesses scurry between the other temples around the plaza.

The markets on either side of the Temple of the Triad are already set up, and more merchants are flooding in to sell their goods.

People flock between the stalls, testing the ripeness of fruit and checking labels on big jugs of wine and olive oil. The chatter of voices rises as they get closer, passing between two of the statues that litter the square.

Titus's class is held in the covered walkway near one of the markets. They're the first ones to arrive after Titus's teacher, who catches their attention and nods at them as they approach.

Titus eases himself down onto a nearby bench. It's hard for him to sit on the ground like many of the other boys.

The teacher changed the location of class to this spot, where Titus could sit on the bench instead.

"Thanks, Fabia," he says, leaning his crutch against the white marble of the bench beside him, just like every morning.

"Have a good day!" she says to Titus with affection, before turning and skipping off across the Forum.

The city has much more action than before. Stores and restaurants open their enormous wooden doors to the street. Workers and artisans bustle down the sidewalks.

Carts rattle through the streets, the drivers shouting at people in frustration to get out of the crossings. The buzz of conversation fills the air, and the smell of fresh bread and hot food wafts over the sidewalks.

Fabia waits for a cart to pass. Then, she quickly hops across the street's crossing stones. She skips around the corner and onto one of the largest streets in the city.

"Morning, Fabia!" a voice calls out from behind a counter.

Fabia grins. It's Julius, who owns one of the best restaurants in Pompeii. She often gets lunch for her father there.

"Morning, Julius!" She pauses at the counter to speak with him.

"Will I be seeing you later today?" Julius asks.

"Of course." Fabia glances at the hot dishes of food in front of her.

The pots are set into the counter, which is laid with colorful fragments of stone. It's not fine mosaic work, like her father does, but it's very bright and eye-catching.

"I will be by to get lunch later." Fabia snatches a dried date from one of the bowls before she leaves. Julius gives her a wink to tell her it's all right.

Fabia makes her way to the bakery that her mother prefers. It is almost all the way across the city from the Forum, close to the arena, where sporting events and gladiator fights are held. Luckily, the city isn't huge, so even going all the way across doesn't take too much time.

The bakery has its usual busyness when Fabia arrives, so she tucks herself back into the corner to wait for it to clear out.

Behind the counter, Felix works quickly to get orders for customers. Everybody who works at the bakery, including Felix, is enslaved.

Fabia's father used to be enslaved, too, but he had been able to train as an artisan and had managed to buy his freedom before he married her mother. Because of this, he has always opposed the slavery system in Rome.

Fabia agrees with him. It's not fair for some people to be free while others are not. If Fabia were in charge, she would change the system.

Finally, the last customer steps back onto the street and Fabia moves toward the counter.

"Morning, Felix," she calls. Felix turns from where he was organizing the racks of hot bread.

"Fabia! My favorite customer." Felix has known her whole family for years, and he and Fabia have always had a great friendship.

"The usual, please." Fabia hands over her basket and Felix takes the coins out before reaching for one of the large, round loaves.

Fabia watches Felix's deft fingers wrap the bread in cloth. He doesn't even startle when the loud sound of a braying donkey comes from the back of the bakery.

Fabia feels sorry for the donkeys, trapped forever having to work inside the bakery. They are tied to the flour grinding stones and have nothing to do but walk around in circles all day long.

Her thoughts are interrupted by another loud donkey bray.

"Everything okay back there?" Fabia asks.

"Been having trouble controlling them lately. All the earthquakes are aggravating them," Felix replies. "You'd think they'd get used to feeling them all the time, but they never do."

"Seems like there have been more lately," Fabia says, trying to peer into the back.

Felix hands the basket to Fabia, two rounds of cloth-wrapped bread tucked neatly inside.

Fabia takes it from him but doesn't leave. Instead, she sets it on the counter, leans on her elbows next to it, and continues the conversation.

"Why do you think the earthquakes happen?" she asks.

"The will of the gods, Fabia," Felix says, glancing at the tiny shrine in the corner of the shop.

The daily offerings are already sitting on it. Felix puts them out every morning to bring good luck and business to the bakery. "Here." He holds out his hand.

"What is it?"

"A treat, for you. Don't tell on me, now."

The bread he places in her hand is still warm, the outside perfectly crispy and the inside perfectly soft. Sweet honey spreads over Fabia's tongue when she takes a bite.

"Delicious," she says, but her mouth is full, and the word comes out muffled.

Felix laughs as Fabia devours the treat and licks the sticky remains of honey off her fingers. The last of the sweetness settles on her tongue, and she savors it for a moment.

She's just about to boost herself onto the counter so she can sit and chat, when she hears her name from behind.

CHAPTER 3

Fabia turns around to see Penelope. Fabia met her when she had helped her father lay the mosaic floors in Penelope's villa.

Penelope's family is very wealthy, and her husband is an important politician in Rome. They're the only family Fabia knows that owns both a home in Rome and a villa outside of Pompeii, on the slopes of the mountain.

Penelope's fine clothes seem almost out of place in the dust of the city. Her hair is swept into a perfect updo.

Standing next to her is her daughter Thalia, who looks identical to Penelope, all the way down to her fancy shoes. She's about the same age as Fabia, but they've barely even exchanged hellos before. Thalia almost never even talks, as far as Fabia can tell. For a long time, Fabia wasn't even sure she could talk.

"Oh, good morning." Fabia quickly takes her hands off the counter.

"How are you today?" Penelope asks politely.

"I'm well, thank you for asking," Fabia replies.

Most of the women from wealthy families don't come into the city to do their own food shopping. Penelope, though, comes in all the time, usually accompanied by a maid, and sometimes by Thalia.

Fabia has seen her at the markets at the Forum and in quite a few shops around the city. She always stops to say hello when she notices Fabia on the street. Her friendliness makes Fabia feel special.

"Your family is well? Titus?"

Fabia's father had been laying the floors in their villa when Titus had his accident all those years ago. Penelope had heard about the cart that broke his leg, and the many days after when they weren't sure if he would survive. Penelope always asks after him.

"Yes, thank you. He's in classes at the Forum," Fabia replies, starting to get antsy.

She doesn't mind the talking. It's the standing still that gets her. She has no idea how Thalia manages to stand so perfectly still behind Penelope all the time.

Just for something to do with her hands, Fabia picks up her basket and fiddles with the woven handle.

"Your father's business is good?"

"Oh yes," Fabia says. "He's laying the mosaics in the Central Baths right now. I've been helping him. Lucius is gone on an apprenticeship to Rome."

She tries to sound proud when she finishes, instead of jealous.

Her older brother is almost as good at laying mosaics as their father, and his apprenticeship is a big step up. Fabia secretly thinks she's even better than him, but no master mosaicist in Rome would take her on as an apprentice.

As a girl, she isn't allowed to go to school. She certainly wouldn't be allowed to follow an artisan career like Lucius.

Fabia is lucky her father even allows her to help him now. She knows that she won't be allowed to for much longer.

As she gets older, she'll have to help her mother at home more so she can learn how to run her own household one day. The thought makes her upset, so she pushes it away. That time's not here yet.

"It must be hard for your father to lose such a skilled worker. Are you still helping him?" Penelope asks.

Penelope never acts like it's strange that Fabia likes working with her father, and never reminds her that she'll have to stop someday.

"Yes, whenever I can." Fabia is about to say more when the ground suddenly trembles underneath them. It only lasts for a couple of seconds, and then, the shaking stops.

The sounds of braying donkeys and shouting men echo from the depths of the bakery behind Felix.

Fabia takes the opportunity to escape Penelope's questions.

"Another earthquake. They're becoming so common lately. I'd better go. Good luck with the donkeys, Felix!" Fabia picks up her basket and heads for the big doors. She gives her friend a wave and nods politely to Penelope and Thalia.

Once she's back on the street, Fabia squeezes past a line of men on the street and turns the corner, headed for home. This side street is much narrower but also less crowded with people.

In the distance, she hears the commotion of the gladiators as they practice just a couple of streets away.

Some mornings, Fabia goes to see them before going home, even though her mother doesn't approve of the games. She and Titus have never been allowed to watch them before, no matter how much they beg.

Fabia likes watching them practice the moves, though. She imagines watching them actually fight in the big amphitheater just behind their training grounds.

Before she can decide if she wants to turn off and visit them before going home, the ground underneath her starts to shake again. She pauses, keeping her balance while she waits for it to stop. Except this time, it doesn't.

CHAPTER 4

Fabia stumbles as the ground rocks beneath her. The cement between the cobblestones cracks with the movement of the earth.

She grabs the handle of her basket more firmly to stop it from swinging and reaches out with her other hand for the house beside her, hoping it will steady her.

Around her, people are shouting and ducking indoors. They seize fragile pottery so it doesn't fall and shatter on the floor, and steady swaying bags of fruit so they don't collide and bruise.

A donkey screams in the distance. The water in a public fountain splashes wildly from side to side. Even the sludge in the middle of the road rocks, creating little waves.

Fabia hears an ominous cracking sound above her.

She glances up just in time to see one of the large clay roof tiles plunging toward her. It barely misses her, instead shattering on the sidewalk directly in front of her. Shards fly in all directions, and Fabia dodges to the side to avoid getting sliced.

There's another crack from above, and Fabia steps even farther back. She is unsteady as the ground moves and is afraid of more falling tiles.

Before she can find shelter under the nearest awning, the earthquake finally slows and comes to a stop.

People around her emerge from shops, some still shouting in fear, others quiet with shock.

Evidence of the earthquake is all around them.

Cracks lace up walls and goods lie spread across shop floors. More than one tile fell, and Fabia can see several more broken all up and down the lane.

She's never felt an earthquake as strong as that before. Nothing that had caused roof tiles to fall and walls to crack. Nothing that had gone on for so long without even a pause.

Quickly, Fabia darts off, heading straight for home. Often earthquakes happen in groups. She's expecting to feel another one any second now. Better to be safe at home than out in the street again with tiles plummeting toward her head.

She keeps glancing up worriedly as she rushes along the sidewalks, remembering the tile that had almost hit her. What if another one is loose and falls even without an earthquake?

As she makes her way home, Fabia watches people sweep pieces of roof tiles off the sidewalk and into the street. Mule drivers are still trying to calm their animals.

She leaps over a large pool of dark wine spreading out of a shop.

When she glances in, she sees that one of the wooden racks that holds the enormous jugs has broken, and the whole shop floor is covered in liquid.

Inside, everybody is talking loudly about the earthquake, worried about damage to buildings and goods.

By the time she arrives at home, there have been no other earthquakes, and her heart has stopped racing as she calms down.

Maybe all the little earthquakes rolled into one big one this time, so no more will be coming after.

"Did you feel the earthquake?" Fabia shouts as she runs into the door of her father's workshop.

A couple of apprentices are at work cutting stone into little cubes just the right size for mosaics.

Later they'll help deliver the cubes to the Central Baths where her father is working. He's been there since early this morning, before Fabia was even awake.

Fabia's mother looks up from where she's bent over a wax tablet, doing the accounts.

"Mother!" Fabia calls, waving at her.

"Did you get the bread?" her mother asks, crossing the room to her.

Fabia hands over the basket. "What about that earthquake?" she says with excitement. "I've never felt one that big!"

It was a bit scary in the moment, especially when the tile fell right next to her. But now that it's over, it feels like an adventure.

"It was pretty big," her mother agrees, quickly checking that the bread is in the basket. "But not as big as the one seventeen years ago. It almost knocked over the Temple of the Triad!"

Fabia nods. She's heard this story before.

That earthquake had leveled whole sections of the city. Most of the buildings around the Forum had been damaged. The government offices had been vacated for months.

Some repairs are still happening to this day, like the ones at the Temple of the Triad. A lot of the damage from that earthquake is still visible, and Pompeii has been under construction for as long as Fabia can remember.

"You off to see your father today?" Fabia's mother asks.

"Yes!" Fabia gives her mother a hug and the apprentices a wave. Then, she darts back out the door onto the busy street, excited to get to work with her father.

The Central Baths are on the main street through the city, not far from Julius's restaurant.

It's not the first time her father has done work on this street. After the big earthquake seventeen years ago, some people used the destruction as an excuse to redo their houses.

That's where Fabia's father had really gotten his start, laying new floors throughout Pompeii.

Now he's one of the most respected mosaicists in the city.

Fabia pauses to let a large group of people pass her and glances into the open door of the house beside her. Inside the home's entryway is the first mosaic that she'd helped her father design.

The mosaic shows a large dog growling with its teeth bared.

Fabia smiles, remembering how the owner had asked her father to make it look like his real-life dog.

It was the first time Fabia had helped her father actually design a mosaic, instead of just laying it.

In Fabia's opinion, it looks a lot fiercer than the real thing, but the man had been very happy with how it turned out.

Once the crowd passes, Fabia darts away again, eager to join her father.

CHAPTER 5

Her father is bent over his unfinished mosaic when Fabia comes skipping into the Central Baths. He's made progress since the day before, but there's still a lot of floor left for them to tile.

"Hello, Father," Fabia says, coming up to peer over his shoulder.

He doesn't respond at first. Instead, he carefully moves a tile slightly to the left so it's in the perfect spot. When he's satisfied, he sits back and rests his dusty hands on his dark tunic, leaving a pale impression of his palms on the fabric.

"Hello, Fabia," he says, smiling with his happiness to see her. "Ready to work?"

"Absolutely!" She joins her father on the floor and looks over his work from the morning.

He's made good progress. Fabia finds where she had left off the day before and takes a moment to look it over. She doesn't want to make any mistakes when she starts laying the tiles into place.

Around her are the noises of construction and shouting workers, but she tunes it all out.

She and her father have been working here for several months, planning and designing the floors for the new public baths.

He's the head mosaicist on the project. Even with the team he's hired, Fabia knows it will probably take them over a year to finish the entire space. She's excited to see how it will look once it's all come together. It's the largest project her father has ever worked on before.

Fabia's fingers find the pattern easily, laying the little tiles out to create interlocking geometric shapes. In the next room, another mosaicist is measuring the area and drawing up plans for the large sea scene that will decorate the whole room, floor to ceiling.

This is the room that Fabia is most looking forward to working on. She thinks with excitement about the delicate mosaics depicting the gods of the sea and the creatures that serve them.

It will be the most finely detailed work she's ever had to do, and she loves thinking about the many people who will see the mosaics once the baths are complete. Since it's a public space, there will be more traffic than in private houses.

As they work, Fabia tells her father about what she saw in the Forum that morning. She also relays the story of how she almost made the jump across the street. He listens on with amusement.

The other workers don't usually pay her any mind. There are no girl apprentices, and she knows they think her father is indulging her by letting her work with him.

Her father always answers her questions without judgment and lets her help with whatever project he's working on. Fabia even feels like he relies on her now, especially with her older brother gone. Lucius had always been supportive of her interest, too. She misses working alongside him.

After a few hours, her father pauses to look out the window, judging the time. The high windows let in sunlight, so the air is clear of torch smoke as they work. The stones and cement glint as they finish each section.

"Think it's about time for lunch?" he asks, and Fabia nods. She drops her remaining tiles back into their bin.

"Julius's?" she asks hopefully. The date she'd taken this morning was very good, and she hopes he still has some left.

Fabia's father hands her a couple of coins. She wraps her fingers around them firmly before heading for the door. She pauses as she steps into the courtyard, letting her eyes adjust to the brightness of the midday sun.

Workers shout to each other across the grounds. They move the large slabs of marble that will eventually make the floors of the baths, or line the large swimming pool being built in the courtyard.

Fabia has barely put a foot out the door when the ground begins to shake underneath her.

She drops the coins as she throws her hands out for balance. They clatter away on the stone floor. This is a much larger earthquake than before. It feels as though a god has seized the city and is shaking it like dice in a hand.

The sounds of alarmed shouts are almost drowned out by the rumbling of buildings as their fixtures grind together. Cracks spread up the plaster covering the walls that surround the courtyard as little fragments flake off.

Above it all, Fabia hears a familiar cracking sound and ducks farther inside without bothering to look up. Around the high sides of the courtyard, she can see roof tiles vibrating and falling off the edges of the building. One smashes on the ground directly in front of Fabia.

All that is drowned out by a deep sound, the loudest Fabia has ever heard. It's more than a sound—almost a feeling, like something moving inside her ears and chest. Her ribcage seems to shake with it, and she feels it in every limb.

Is this what the gods sound like when they speak? Everyone is startled silent by it, and the shaking of the ground slows.

Nervously, Fabia steps outside again, quickly moving away from the walls of the buildings. She looks around for the source of the noise.

The workers are doing the same as they stare into the distance and point above the roof, toward Mount Vesuvius.

Fabia looks into the distance and gasps.

CHAPTER 6

Black smoke is rising from the top of the mountain. It is more smoke than Fabia has ever seen in her life. It pours into the sky, quickly forming a darkness above Vesuvius.

"Fabia!"

Fabia turns at the sound of her name to see her father looking around for her frantically.

"Father!" she calls, and he dashes over to her, gathering her up in a tight hug. "Look." Fabia points to the mountain.

He lets go of her and looks at where she's pointing, one hand resting on her shoulder. Behind her, she hears a thunderous *crash* as a pile of stones falls over. Beyond the walls of the bathhouse, Fabia can hear people shouting in the streets. She's sure all of them have the same astonished feeling she has.

The ground shakes again but not as strongly. Fabia watches as more smoke erupts from Vesuvius. The cloud of smoke is moving quickly across the sky and toward Pompeii. The day around them begins to darken.

"We have to get out!" one of the workers calls, and the men stampede for the gates to the bath.

Fabia's father doesn't move at first. Then, he reaches his hand out to the sky. Something pale settles on his skin. Fabia looks at it closely. It's gray ash.

"What's happening to Vesuvius?" she asks her father.

"Nothing good," he says, frowning.

The ground shakes, and Fabia feels that deep rumble again, vibrating in her chest and ears. The top of the mountain seems to explode upward, the column in the sky growing larger

and darker. Already the ash is falling more thickly. For a moment, Fabia wonders if the whole mountain is going to burst into the sky and come raining down on the city.

"Go!" her father says, giving her shoulder a push and startling her into motion. They follow the rest of the workers toward the gate.

The street is packed full of people. Many are panicking, shoving at each other as they search for a way out.

Fabia shrinks away from the commotion, her heart racing.

Fabia's father shakes her to get her attention. "Fabia, you have to get out of the city."

Before she can respond, one of the workers behind her scoffs. "No. This will be over soon. Better to hide inside until the mountain has worn itself out."

"No!" another one says. "He's right. We'll have no chance of survival if we stay.

Who knows what's happening, or when it will stop?"

Fabia's father ignores the argument and keeps his eyes fixed on Fabia. "Go get Titus and both of you get out of Pompeii." He glances at the street, then north toward the mountain. People are moving toward the harbor along both main streets, like a river of bodies pouring toward the sea. "Go east," he says sharply. "Take the Nola Gate and keep walking as far as you can. Do not stop."

"That's stupid," the man next to him says. "Obviously, these people have the right idea. Ships are the fastest way out of the city if you're going to leave."

Fabia's father is already shaking his head before the man has stopped speaking. "You think they'll let any of us on a ship? No, it will be the rich who get out, and they will leave the rest of us on the shore at the mercy of

Vesuvius. Your best option is to escape on foot, and the only way that will take you away from the mountain is east, inland. Fabia, go get Titus and get out."

"What about you?" Fabia cries. She grips him tightly as the ground shakes again. People on the street scream and shove each other harder. Fear and dismay fill Fabia's face as she glances

between them and her father. She doesn't want to leave him and be all alone in the panicking crowd.

"I will go get your mother, and we'll meet you on the road. You must be brave, Fabia. You can do that for me, right?"

Fabia nods and swallows hard, trying to force down her nervousness. "Okay," she says shakily.

Her father pulls her into one more tight hug before releasing her. "I love you. I will see you soon. Now go!"

With one last terrified look, Fabia steps out into the street.

CHAPTER 7

Immediately, Fabia is swept up by the crowd rushing down the sidewalk. Luckily, it's going in the direction she is, so she lets it take her along instead of trying to fight it.

The crush of people is hot and rough, and Fabia knows she can't stay in the crowd for long.

She shoves her way closer to the street than the wall. She can't let the panic distract her. She has to get to Titus quickly.

At the first opportunity, she hops across the crossing stones, relieved to be out of the pack of bodies. She has already forgotten her game from this morning. There was no time for silly games anymore.

Fabia chances a look down the street, toward Julius's restaurant. Through a rare division in the crowd, she spots the counter. It is cracked down the middle. The stack of bowls that had sat at one end is gone, probably toppled over in the earthquake. There's no sign of Julius or any of his customers or employees.

Someone knocks against her, and she barely catches her balance. Lots of people are running through the brown muck in the road. It is more full than normal with the water spilling out of the public fountains. It splashes up, and Fabia finishes crossing the street quickly, trying to avoid it.

The side street she turns onto is much quieter, and Fabia lets out a long breath she hadn't realized she was holding. It's good to be away from the crowd. Most people are headed for the larger thoroughfares to escape the city.

The ground is littered with trash, broken pieces of doors, or spilled food. One of the balconies has collapsed, spreading rubble and broken wood into the street.

Fabia has to climb over it carefully to avoid splinters and sharp pieces of brick.

Some of the shops are empty of people, with only food and tools left lying abandoned on tables or scattered on the floor. In others, the owners are trying to shut the doors to the street.

Fabia glances up at the black cloud. Ash is still falling gently from the sky, but at ground level it's being quickly swept away by either the water from the fountains or the movement of people. Higher up, it's beginning to settle in a layer on the edges of roofs.

The cloud itself has gotten even larger. More and more smoke is pouring from the top of Vesuvius. Fabia's chest tightens with anxiety, and she has to remind herself to breathe and stay focused. She just has to get to Titus.

Then, once they are together, they can get out of the city and meet Mother and Father.

Fabia rounds the final corner, then skids to a halt just as a panicked mule dashes in front of her, its eyes wild with fear. It's gone in an instant, headed across the Forum, in the opposite direction of the mountain. Fabia follows behind it, coming around the corner of the Temple of the Triad. She starts scanning the crowd, desperately looking around for her brother.

The Forum is madness. Stalls and carts are abandoned, collapsed, or overturned. Goods spill across the smooth white stones, and a few of the statues have fallen and shattered. Their surfaces are brightly painted, but Fabia can see the pale flash of marble from where they've broken. Olive oil spreads in yellow-green pools around toppled pottery. Ash is gathering on the slick, smooth surface.

A crowd has gathered in the center of the Forum, staring and pointing at the mountain, even as the daylight fades under the cloud. Around them, people and animals dash back and forth, trying desperately to find the best escape route.

Titus's class is not where they usually meet, under the balcony by the markets. Fabia's heart skips a beat. Where did they go? She has no idea how she'll find Titus in the crowds with all the commotion and chaos.

She takes another few steps, then pauses, staring around. It's getting difficult to differentiate people as the ash grows thicker. Everyone is turning a ghostlike gray with streaks of color where they've brushed the ash off.

Fabia watches as people climb the steps to the Temple of the Triad and disappear between the columns.

Fabia lets out a sharp breath as she spots a small figure with a crutch just cresting the top stair. A brown leather bag hangs from his shoulder. That must be Titus!

She takes off toward him, dodging other people and leaping over obstacles. Fabia's lungs are burning as she runs as fast as she can through the mass of bodies. She finds a gap and races up the stairs, trying not to slip on the stone worn smooth from centuries of feet climbing it.

Titus is gathered with his classmates around their teacher, just under the cover of the

temple roof. He leans heavily against one of the columns, breathing hard, and just barely manages not to fall as the ground shakes again.

"We have displeased the gods!" the teacher shouts, and his terrified students nod along in agreement. "The city has been neglectful of the gods, and this is their judgment. The only way to save the city is to appease them!"

"Titus!" Fabia cries out as she reaches the top of the steps.

Her brother turns his head in surprise at the sound of her cry. "Fabia?"

"We must pray and make offerings," Titus's teacher continues. "We must show them that we respect their power. Only then will they calm the mountain!"

Fabia ignores the teacher. "Are you okay?" She reaches for Titus's hand with affection, feeling a sudden need to touch him and make sure he's real.

"It seems like the world is ending," Titus says as he glances back at his teacher, who is still ranting about the gods.

"We've got to go." Fabia tugs on Titus, turning back toward the stairs. She knows that staying put like this won't do them any good. "Father told me to get you and get out of the city." She looks over his shoulder at his classmates, seemingly frozen in place. "You should get out of here!" she yells at the assembled group, but none of them respond.

"Let's go." Titus puts his weight back on his crutch, and together they move out of the protection of the columns.

Fabia spares one last glance over her shoulder at the students and Titus's still-ranting teacher before turning away.

CHAPTER 8

The Forum is just as chaotic as before, and Fabia keeps Titus close to the wall of the temple, guiding him north.

She doesn't want to get separated from him by venturing too far from the protection of the building.

"Toward the mountain?" Titus asks, staring wide-eyed at the thickness of the smoke cloud that's now covering the city.

"We're going out the Nola Gate," Fabia says. She's leading them toward the main east-west road that runs straight to the gate. It will be the fastest way out of the city.

Except when they get there, the road is just as packed as the north-south one that Fabia had crossed to get to the Forum. The crowd is still swelling even larger as more people are fleeing. Most of the crowd is flowing west, toward the water and the ships.

For a moment, Fabia is tempted to join them. It would be easier. The ships would be faster. But then, she remembers what her father said. Even if they could get there, nobody would take them aboard.

"Fabia..." Titus says, nudging her. "I can't..."

"I know." Even if the crowds were going in the right direction, Titus probably couldn't manage it. There are too many people, moving too fast and with too little regard for each other.

"We have to find a different way around," Titus says. His knuckles are white where they grip the shaft of his crutch.

Fabia nods. Together they turn and go back the way they came to find another option.

They turn at the arched entrance of the Forum and take a smaller street east.

The ground rumbles again, and the walls above them creak ominously. There are people on this street, too. But there are fewer, and not all of them are moving in the same direction. Some seem to be preparing to hunker down and stay, like those Fabia had seen earlier.

Something hard and sharp hits Fabia's head and she jumps, startled. She looks up, expecting to see the wall of a building coming down on her.

"What was that?" she asks as she hears the sound of stones hitting the ground. It doesn't look like any of the buildings are collapsing.

"Look." Titus stoops down, picking up something small and dark. He holds it out in his hand for Fabia to see.

It looks like a rock, but it is full of holes lined in sharp edges. When Fabia takes it from him, it weighs almost nothing. She handles it delicately so as not to cut her fingers on it.

"What is that?" she asks.

Titus shakes his head. Just like her, he has no idea. Another rock hits Titus's shoulder and bounces to the ground.

Fabia feels a sharp pain in her forehead and raises her hand. One of the rocks hits her, leaving a small cut behind.

"We can't just stand here," Titus says. "Let's keep moving."

Fabia spots a large, thin piece of wood in the street. It looks like a broken shutter. She picks it up and holds it over them for protection against the falling rocks as they continue down the street.

More rocks are falling, but not steadily. They come in fits and starts, but still, they begin to build up on the street.

Fabia and Titus move with caution as they try not to slip. The rocks look delicate with all their lacy holes, but they're sturdy and don't break or crack when stepped on.

After what feels like an eternity, they reach the main road. They stop at the corner, trying to catch their breath.

The awning above them blocks the little rocks, but they can still hear them pinging off the roof and clattering to the ground. It sounds like rain, but the hardest rain Fabia could imagine.

The street is slightly emptier, but now, people are carrying bags and baskets stuffed full. Some are so large that people are dragging them. Most of the shops along the street have been closed up, the large wooden panels moved into place in front of the entrances.

In the windows overlooking the street, Fabia can see frightened faces looking out over the action happening below them.

The road is filled with a mixture of muck, ash, and rocks.

As she looks down the street, she notices Julius. Julius's hands shake as he and a waiter move the painted wooden doors into place to protect the shop and his livelihood.

He looks up and spots Fabia. He says something to one of the waiters, then rushes down the street to join her and Titus under the awning.

"Do you need a place to hide?" he asks, looking at them with a sense of protection. "Some people from the neighborhood are inside, keeping safe."

Behind him, a crowd of anxious faces appears from the darkness of his restaurant.

One person tugs impatiently on the sleeve of the waiter's tunic. They're asking him to finish closing up the building, pointing at the mountain and shouting in desperation.

"Father told us to get out of the city," Fabia says, though she must admit the thought of taking shelter at the restaurant is tempting. The taste of the date from this morning is gone from her mouth, but she remembers it.

Julius has the essentials for survival, food and probably water inside. And the building seems sturdy enough. Strong enough to withstand a mountain, though? Fabia is not sure.

Julius gestures around in disbelief. "Surely he must not have meant for his children to be running around out here."

Fabia glances at Titus, who shakes his head. "No, we should get out," he says softly, then louder, again to Julius.

The man looks back at his restaurant, where the door is half-moved into place. If he doesn't get back inside soon, he'll be shut out.

"Good luck, kids," he says, already backing up. A few seconds later, the door is closed on him and the people in his restaurant.

CHAPTER 9

"C'mon, we have to go," Titus says, shifting his attention to the street in front of them.

"You ready?" Fabia asks Titus.

"Yes. Ready as I'll ever be," he says with determination. He shifts his bag up on his shoulder.

For a moment, Fabia wants to suggest that he leave the bag, but she decides not to. The bag and the tablet were expensive, and they're the best tools Titus has. There's no way she can ask him to leave them behind.

They cross the street as quickly as they're able, Titus in front. Fabia stops on the center crossing stone. She looks down the street in hopes of seeing her father. There's nobody she recognizes, but it's hard to tell who's who in the increasing dark and rain of rocks.

Fabia glances in the other direction, toward the baths where she'd worked with her father earlier that day. No sign of him there, either. As she watches, a small child runs into the complex, probably looking for a safe location to hide.

Above the buildings, Vesuvius continues to produce smoke, and occasional small earthquakes shake the ground.

The moment in the Forum this morning feels like a lifetime ago, when Fabia had thought of the mountain as a home for the gods. Now, it feels more like the gods' war zone. Her beloved city is no more than an insignificant casualty of the gods' fury.

Fabia swallows hard, tamping down on the fear she feels rising inside her. No, she can't let it overwhelm her. She has a job to do. Get out of the city.

"Is this the right way?" Titus asks once they've crossed the intersection and are once again on a side street.

"Yes," Fabia responds.

Even though most of Pompeii is laid out in a grid, it can be easy to get lost on the streets. Sometimes, a street you think is running straight is slightly slanted, and you end up somewhere you didn't expect. But Fabia has been all over the city with her father. She knows the streets well.

"Father did some work down here last year. I was with him. This road will get us closer to the gate."

They make their way down the sidewalk, but it's getting more difficult to see. It feels like late evening as the sun is covered by the clouds of smoke and ash from Vesuvius, even though it's barely afternoon.

The sidewalk is covered in pebbles. At one point, Fabia and Titus have to move into the middle of the street and wade through them to get around a collapsed balcony.

Fabia feels the sharp edges of the pebbles scraping around her sandals at the skin of her feet. Still, she doesn't stop moving. She's worried that if she does, she won't have the strength of will to start back up again.

More ash falls from the sky. It builds up in piles on every surface and is soft when Fabia tries touching it. It sticks to her skin in a way that's so unpleasant she has to brush her hands on her tunic repeatedly in an effort to get it off. Even then, she can still feel the residue coating her.

The two of them don't speak except to offer each other help. Fabia does her best to keep the wooden shutter over them both as protection from falling rocks.

After a while, her arms ache with exhaustion from the effort of holding it up. When the ground shakes again, she drops it and almost loses her balance.

She reaches for Titus's shoulder, and her fingers tighten when there's another roar from Vesuvius. The world gets even darker, or so it seems to Fabia.

"We'll turn here," Fabia says, pointing to the intersection ahead of them.

Their eyes have adjusted somewhat to the gloom. The world is painted strangely flat by the ash still coming down like snow from above.

Fabia recognizes this intersection well. One of the corner houses had redone their floors last year and had hired Fabia's father to lay them.

Fabia loved that job, in particular, for the variety of colors used in the mosaics.

It was a collection of large squares, each one containing a different image inside. Some were flowers or animals. But others were complex gladiatorial fights, or celebrations of food, all bordered by tiles laid out to look like a twisted rope.

Fabia had loved the visual effect and had spent many hours looking at the designs in amazement.

She pauses at the corner, staring across at the tightly closed door and the mosaics hidden behind it. For a brief, sharp moment, she longs to see them again. The longing is cut off as the ground shakes under them.

A loud crack comes from the building at the corner of the intersection.

Like in a dream, Fabia sees it sway and then start to topple.

The front wall falls outward as the painted plaster surface cracks and the cement between the bricks comes apart.

She sees it all as if in slow motion, the slow swaying and fracturing of the building as it descends toward the ground.

Titus is standing ahead of Fabia, almost directly in its path.

"Titus!" Fabia dashes forward between Titus and the building.

She pushes him back. He stumbles, almost losing his grip on his crutch.

Fabia registers the look of shock and fear on his face before the building comes down on top of her.

CHAPTER 10

Fabia opens her eyes, but her vision is clouded in darkness.

She hears the sound of her name being called, faint and distant, over the constant rumble of the mountain. She turns her head in confusion, looking for the source. What happened? Where is she?

For a few uncertain moments she thinks she must be dead, and this is the path to the underworld.

"Fabia!" Titus's face appears out of the gloom, his expression full of nervousness.

"Titus?"

"You're alive," he cries as his reaction turns to relief. "Are you hurt?"

Fabia moves one arm, then the other. Then, she moves both of her legs. Nothing seems damaged badly, though she certainly doesn't feel normal. "I don't think anything's broken," she says. "What happened?"

"The building fell on you," he says. "I think that beam protected you, but I can't lift it. Can you crawl out?"

Fabia reaches out, feeling around her and trying to get her bearings from inside the pile of rubble. The crossbeam that Titus mentioned is slanted upward. One end rests on the ground and the other on a pile of bricks and plaster from the collapsed wall.

Titus peers in at her through a small gap in the bricks. It's just large enough of a space for them to talk through, but not large enough for her to escape.

Balanced on the beam are the large wooden door panels from the building. They made a little pocket of safety under the beam, giving her protection from the rest of the building. It's a wonder she did survive. Without the beam, she would have certainly been crushed. But now, she's trapped.

When she pushes on the wooden panels, they hardly move. Neither do the bricks beside the gap that Titus is looking through.

"I don't think I can squeeze out," she says after trying for a moment. "Maybe if we can lift this panel, there will be enough space."

Titus puts one shoulder to it, and on the count of three, they shove upward as hard as they can.

Fabia can hear the debris above her rattle and move. It echoes in her cavern. The panel lifts a little, but the gap still isn't large enough for Fabia.

"I have an idea," Titus says. But before Fabia can ask him what it is, he's disappeared from view.

All alone, Fabia does her best to try and stay calm. But she can't help but think about the worst-case scenario. What if she really is stuck and they can't get her out? What if another building collapses?

Thankfully, Titus reappears a moment later and wedges the end of his crutch under the panel. "A lever," he says, grinning. "Let's try again, okay?"

"All right." Fabia positions herself as close to the gap as she can, and on Titus's count of three, she shoves up again while Titus presses down on the end of his crutch.

The panel lifts up, farther this time. There's a loud clatter as something large rolls off the wood.

"Come on!" Titus shouts, and Fabia slides out of the space and back onto the street.

The panel clatters down behind her as Titus releases the lever. Fabia sits up, and Titus drops to his knees beside her in exhaustion.

Fabia grabs him in a hug, clinging to him tightly in relief. "That was a good idea," she says. She tries to take a deep breath to calm her racing heart, but instead she coughs on the ash lingering in the air.

Titus sits beside her, also coughing. He's breathing hard, hands shaking, though Fabia can't tell if it's from exertion or fear.

"Thanks for saving me," she says, scooting so their shoulders are touching.

"Anytime," he says back, leaning a little on her. "Just give me a minute, okay?"

"I think I need one, too," Fabia responds.

They sit quietly. Fabia stares at the pile of rubble that almost buried her. The walls that were both her trap and her protection were the same ones that had surrounded her as she had helped her father lay those beautiful floors.

Never had she imagined that the building would, or even *could*, collapse like that. The big earthquakes of the past had been distant stories. Now they're so real Fabia almost can't remember the world before.

After a minute, Titus's chest stops heaving quite so hard, and the tightness in Fabia's limbs eases. She climbs to her feet and holds out a hand for Titus.

The way they'd planned to go is blocked, the building making it impassable.

"We have to go around," Titus says.

Fabia looks down the street. There's another intersection pretty close, but Fabia can barely make it out through the gloom.

The street is empty of people, except sometimes, she thinks she sees an ash-gray shadow moving ahead of them. Each time she does, she hopes it is her parents, but it never is. It's a thin hope. Out of all the streets for them to take, it's unlikely that they would take this one. Fabia clings to it anyway.

She wants to shout and call out their names, but there's no way anyone would hear her over the ongoing thunder of the mountain. It's hard even to hear Titus sometimes, and he's right beside her.

Their only choice is to keep going. Once they are out of the city and on the road, they are sure to meet up with their parents again.

Finally, they turn east again, but more buildings have collapsed, partially blocking the street. They have to slow down to clamber over the destruction of awnings and walls.

The little stones continue to fall. They cover the road, adding to the hardship of their journey. In some places, they are almost a foot deep and roll off the roofs to gather in piles along the sidewalks.

Fabia and Titus help each other over the bigger obstacles, Fabia holding Titus's crutch when he needs both hands to balance. They make slow progress down the street.

Fabia is so focused on putting one foot in front of another that when she steps down into water, it takes her a moment to realize what's happening.

The public fountain has stopped running, but the basin remains full. It had been invisible under the stones that were floating on top, hiding the water.

Fabia picks one up. It's the same as the sharp, porous ones that have been falling from the sky. What kind of rocks float? The water underneath is full of ash and debris.

She's suddenly aware of a burning thirst in the back of her throat. There's no way she'll drink the water here, though. It's thick with ash and dirt, and full of the floating rocks.

Then, there's a loud clatter behind her and a shout of fear.

CHAPTER 11

Titus is curled in a ball on the ground, his shoulders shaking. When Fabia notices, she drops the floating rock and rushes over to crouch by him.

"Titus! Are you okay?" she asks.

"I tripped," Titus replies. He uncurls a little, then holds out his hands to show her.

The heels and palms of his hands are scraped raw and bloody, dark grit spotting the injury. The pop of red blood seems out of place in the increasingly colorless world around them.

"It's okay, Titus," Fabia says automatically. "It's okay."

"No, it's not," Titus argues in frustration. He slowly lifts himself up so he's sitting, and

Fabia can see that he's scraped up his knees, too. "I can't hold my crutch like this."

Fabia shakes her head, already knowing what he's going to say next. "I'm not going to leave you."

"You have to," Titus protests. "I'm just slowing you down. You won't get out if you're trying to get me out. I know you're already moving slower because of me. You could have been out of the city by now."

Gently, Fabia takes his hands in hers, gazing at the scrapes and dirt.

Tears build in her eyes and blur her vision. She blinks them back fiercely, trying not to be overcome with emotion. "No! You didn't leave me. And I'm not going to leave you. We can wrap your hands."

"With what?" Titus asks, gesturing around at the desolate street.

With sudden inspiration, Fabia reaches for the hem of her tunic and tears. It doesn't come apart easily, but eventually, she manages to get two long strips. She wraps them tightly around Titus's hands, ignoring his hisses of pain, and ties the ends together to hold them in place.

"Try it." She helps Titus to his feet and hands him the crutch.

Gingerly, he wraps a hand around it and takes a step. He moves the bottom of the crutch

carefully through the stones, not lifting it all the way.

He nods at Fabia, giving her a tight-lipped smile trying to hide his pain. "Let's go."

Fabia leads the way again, but soon, they come across an impassable junction. "Are you serious?" Fabia says in exasperation, staring at the pile of rubble in front of them.

It used to be a building, but now, it's an obstruction preventing them from turning northward, toward the gate.

It feels like every time she blinks, something else is getting in their way, like the city is trying to keep them trapped.

"Are we going to go around again?" Titus asks.

Fabia sizes up the pile, then shakes her head. "I think we can climb over this. See?" she points to a series of fragments arranged almost like stairs. "Let's try it."

She leads Titus up the pile, testing each spot carefully before she puts her full weight on it.

At the top of the rubble, she looks down the other side, searching for a safe path. She thinks she sees one and turns around to help pull Titus up to join her.

The ground shakes under her, strong and fierce. She shouts in fear, losing her balance.

The condition of the rubble is very unstable. The slab she's standing on begins to slide down. She is shifting away from the top of the pile and Titus.

She crouches, trying desperately not to fall and be crushed beneath the moving rubble. The slab stops at the base and Fabia takes a deep breath, relieved to have made it alive.

There's a groan and a creak above her. It is a sound she's now very familiar with. Without thinking, she throws herself out of the way as another wall comes down.

Fabia scrambles to her feet, taking another few steps just in case it's not done moving.

She turns around to find that the pile is larger now, and definitely unstable.

Some of the wooden beams shift as she watches, and a small shower of bricks rains down onto the street.

"Titus!" Fabia shouts over the pile, looking for any sign that her brother is alive.

Fabia thinks about the likelihood of Titus surviving such a crash. It is essential to find him as soon as possible.

She tries putting her weight on the rubble, but it moves unsteadily under her, and she quickly steps off.

She calls her brother's name again, listening carefully for a response. She thinks she hears her name, but it is faint, almost drowned out by the mountain.

"Go around!" she yells as loudly as she can. "I'll meet you at the next street."

She has to pause to cough through the thick ash. She repeats her words with a sense of desperation, hoping at least a few got through to Titus.

Through the darkness and dust-choked air, she thinks she hears Titus respond, but it's not clear.

Fabia repeats the message one final time. Then, she turns to look at the road ahead of her.

She doesn't want to leave Titus behind her, but she can't get to him here. The only way to find him is to leave the pile behind.

CHAPTER 12

The rest of the street is relatively clear. She moves fast along the sidewalk and reaches the intersection in what feels like record time. The cross street is so narrow that it's all sidewalk, more like an alley than a full street.

There are no crossing stones at this intersection, and it's too dark for her to see much farther up the block. She doesn't have time to go searching for another set.

Fabia is just about to step down into the street to cross when she notices that the stones are moving oddly, rippling up and down like the ground underneath them is breathing somehow. She bends down to check and realizes that there's water running under them. The current is fast and strong.

She looks around for the source and notices another public fountain. This one, like the previous one, is broken. Instead of it having no water, though, it's pouring water, overfilling the sides of the basin and flowing into the street.

Fabia doesn't want to step down into the water. There's no telling what's in it, or exactly how strong the current is. What would happen to Titus if she were swept away?

Fabia eyes up the sidewalk on the other side of the street. She'd made a jump like this just this morning. Never mind that Titus had to stop her from falling in. Fabia knows she can do this.

She breathes as deeply as she can without triggering another coughing fit and fixes her eyes on her landing spot. It's covered in the sharp, light stones that keep falling from the sky.

She's not sure about landing on those, but this is her best option.

One more breath, a step, and she pushes off. The sidewalk is getting closer...closer. For a single, heart-stopping moment, Fabia thinks she's misjudged and won't make it. Then, her feet make contact with the pavement.

The stones roll under her feet and she leans forward, arms spinning before she finally catches herself on the wall. Fabia gives herself one brief moment to celebrate her achievement before she rushes down the alley to the next street. She still needs to get to Titus and get out of the city.

Once she arrives at the intersection of the next road, she looks back south, down the road for Titus. But the day has gotten even darker under the sky of falling ash. It no longer feels like day at all, though it was barely past noon

when Vesuvius erupted. The street is empty. There's no motion. All she sees are shadows.

This street, like the other one, is mostly clear of destroyed buildings, with just a few collapsed awnings and the ever-growing piles of floating stones. It won't take her long to go down and find Titus. She can't just leave him.

Fabia is about to head down the street when she sees movement ahead of her. She shouts in excitement. The figure moves toward her and her heart leaps. Is it Titus?

But no, the figure is too tall. Fabia pauses, unsure whether she wants to keep going or shrink back. The figure, pale with the ash covering him, stops in front of her. He leans forward, squinting through the darkness.

"Fabia?"

Fabia startles, then looks closer. "Felix?"

Felix pulls off the piece of cloth he has covering his lower face, and his features

suddenly become clear. It's such a wonderful relief to see a familiar face in all this unfamiliar destruction that Fabia wants to hug him.

"What are you doing here?" he asks with the same astonishment as she feels.

"Titus and I, we got separated trying to get out." She peers around him down the street. "I'm trying to find him."

Felix looks over his shoulder, then back at Fabia. "Titus is here?"

"Yes, coming this way. Hopefully."

Felix kneels down in front of her. Fabia hadn't quite realized just how tall he is, since she's mostly seen him standing behind the counter at the bakery or leaning on it to chat with her. "Fabia, I just came up that road. Titus isn't back there."

Fabia's heart seizes in her chest. "No! I told him to. He's coming this way." She'd heard him call back to her over the rubble. She had!

"No, he's not. Come with me. You and I need to get out of the city while we still can."

Fabia flinches. "I know he's back there, and I won't leave without him."

"Fabia—" Felix tries again, but Fabia shoves him away.

"You don't have to help," she says, suddenly furious. "I'll get him on my own." She pushes past him and begins the trek down the road, not bothering to look back at Felix.

"Fabia," she hears his voice behind her,

but she doesn't turn around. "I don't want to leave you."

"Titus!" she calls into the dark, ignoring Felix. It doesn't matter if he doesn't want to leave her, because there's no way she'll leave her brother. Felix can make the decision to go if he wants to. She doesn't need his help. She'll find her brother on her own. They made it this far together.

"Titus!" She startles at Felix's shout behind her, then feels his hand on her shoulder. He's looking down at her with a grim but determined expression. "Let's go get him."

CHAPTER 13

Fabia and Felix move down the block together, shouting for Titus, trying not to trip over debris or rubble in the gloom. They've made it about halfway down when Fabia hears her own name called back.

Titus is sitting on a fallen column. His face is pale and bloodless even under the ash.

Fabia dashes toward him. Her eyes start to tear up as a wave of relief at having found him washes through her. He did it! He survived and they're back together, just like they should be. And they're so close to getting out.

"What happened?" she asks, looking him over.

"I fell again. My ankle...I can barely walk on it." He gestures to his leg, the one that had been broken when he was little.

Fabia gently reaches down to touch it, trying to see how badly he's hurt. The joint is swollen, puffy, and hot under her fingers. Titus cries out when she tries to bend it, and she quickly lets go.

"You've got your crutch, though," she says desperately.

Titus motions to it, resting against the column beside him. "Broken."

Fabia looks down and can see that almost a foot has snapped off the end. It's far too short for Titus to use now. It would be more of a hindrance than a help.

A tiredness invades Fabia's bones, dragging her down. After all their effort and struggle, after getting almost all the way across the city, she doesn't want it to end like this. It can't end like this!

The destruction is getting worse, and every time the earth moves underneath them, she imagines the walls of the buildings swaying, threatening to topple over.

They're running out of time to get out. Fabia glances over her shoulder up the street. Even though it's dark, she knows that the gate is up ahead, just around the corner.

She'd almost be able to see it, if smoke wasn't obscuring the sun.

"We can do it," she says, trying not to let her desperation creep into her voice. "Come on, I can help you walk."

Titus just shakes his head. "You know that won't work—"

"I can't leave you!" The words come out of her mouth like an explosion, uncontrolled and raw. She looks up at Titus, sees the sadness in his eyes. Little flecks of ash rest on his eyelashes, and more drift down from his hair. "We're going to get out of here together. We have to," Fabia declares.

"Here." Felix puts a hand on Fabia's shoulder. She'd forgotten he was there and almost jumps out of her skin at the contact. "I've got this," Felix says as he gently guides her out of the way and takes her place crouching

in front of Titus. "I can carry you, if that's all right."

Fabia is relieved he joined her, grateful for his helpfulness.

Felix pauses, waiting for Titus's nod of approval. His arms, strong from years of hard work in the bakery, scoop Titus up like he weighs nothing at all.

Fabia follows Felix and Titus up the street. Felix moves slowly and carefully so as not to jostle Titus too much.

Though their eyes have adjusted to the darkening cloud of smoke over the course of the day, there's very little light to brighten their way, so they have to step cautiously. They feel ahead of themselves for obstructions as they wade through the ever-deeper piles of stones raining from the sky.

Around them, Fabia can hear roofs groaning as the weight of the stones increases. More than once, she hears the cracking sound of a roof caving in.

During one, Fabia thinks she catches a high-pitched cut-off scream. Each individual stone might be light, but this large collection of stones must weigh more than the buildings can take.

When they make it to the main road, they spot other people for the first time in a while. After the desolation and emptiness of the streets they'd just come from, seeing so many people is startling.

For a moment, Fabia feels like they can't be real, like there can't still be this many people left in the city when she and Titus were utterly alone for most of their journey.

Caked in ash and grime, people trudge singly or in groups. The initial feeling of panic is gone, but now, there is a sense of exhaustion and desperation to find safety.

Some people carry torches or lanterns, cupping the flames carefully to keep them alive. After the darkness of the smoke-filled air, the lights are blinding. The flames are fragile, though. Even as she watches, one of the lamps is struck by a falling stone and the light disappears.

Fabia peers at faces wherever she can, hoping to see her parents. Nobody looks familiar, though.

She feels a fullness in her throat when she thinks about the last time she saw her mother, in the workshop that very morning. It feels like a lifetime ago.

She wants to go back to the beginning of the day, live it all over again, and make different decisions. Her family wouldn't be separated. They'd all get out together. The last time she saw her father, he swept her up into a hug that felt like safety. Will she ever feel safe like that again? Will she ever see either of their smiles again?

CHAPTER 14

The three of them join the trickle of people heading up the road and toward the gate in the hopes of survival.

When they arrive at the gate, a passing torch illuminates the stern face of the goddess Minerva carved into the top of the arch.

Fabia's father had told her that it was there to give protection to the city and keep the citizens safe. Minerva watched over everyone as they left the city and welcomed them back when they returned.

Fabia pauses in the middle of the road and stares up at the emotionless rock. She can't hide her feelings of betrayal and aggravation.

Minerva was asked to give the city protection, and instead, she's watching it collapse around her. She should have stopped this and kept her people safe.

Fabia bares her teeth, like the goddess is actually there in front of her.

She and Titus have survived all the trials that Vesuvius and Pompeii together have thrown at them. If the gods are trying to kill them, they'll have to try harder.

With one last rebellious look, she passes under the heavy, sturdy stones of the arch and finally leaves the city.

The road beyond the gate is far safer than the city streets. There are no narrow roads with collapsing buildings to threaten them. But the ground still shakes with occasional earthquakes, though Fabia notices that they're less strong now.

Small stones still rain down on them. But the passage of so many people has kept the road mostly clear, shoving the stones off to the side.

Felix stops and lowers Titus to the ground, gently placing him on his feet. Titus reaches out to Fabia for support, and she wraps an arm around him.

"Can you walk from here?" Felix asks in exhaustion. "I don't know if I can carry you much farther. I'm sorry."

Fabia recognizes Titus's look of stubbornness and determination.

"I'll do it," he says, and Fabia lets him lean on her as he takes the first tentative step. He winces but manages not to cry out, and they begin their slow progress up the road.

Now that they're out of the heart-pounding danger, Fabia begins to feel the sharp pain of her injuries. The little cuts and scrapes from climbing over rocks and debris burn. The bruises from the building collapse ache.

Her mouth is overcome by dryness. What she wouldn't give for a cup of water and a bath, followed by a deep sleep in her own bed. But all of that is probably destroyed by now, so Fabia shoves these thoughts to the back of her mind.

The sadness that threatens to overwhelm her is too big to deal with along with everything else.

Many people pass the three of them, but Felix is still sticking close and being a helper to Titus and Fabia wherever he can.

The other people are as unrecognizable here as they were in the city. Their skin, clothes, and hair are all covered in the blank gray of falling ash. Fabia glances at Titus, seeing the ash caught even in his eyelids. They all must look like walking ghosts.

The road begins to slope up, the stones falling less frequently. Fabia is not sure how long they struggle along before she has to pause to breathe. The sky is slightly lighter here, and Fabia realizes they must be reaching the edge of the smoke cloud.

She looks back toward the city. They're high enough now that she can see the last rays of bright, early evening sunlight beyond the cloud of smoke.

It is glittering off the water in the sea. The water in the bay has an unusual thickness, and Fabia rubs her eyes to make sure there's nothing in them. She wouldn't be surprised if they were covered in fine ash.

"It's the rocks," Titus says from beside her. "They're clogging up the water. I don't know if any of the ships can get out of the harbor. And if anybody was trying to rescue us..." He trails off.

Fabia knows what he means. There's no way any ship would approach the city as it is.

The earth shakes under them again, the feeling so routine that Fabia almost doesn't notice. She looks over at Mount Vesuvius, dominating the landscape.

Its slopes used to be covered in olive groves, vineyards, and the summer houses of the rich people from Rome.

Now, it's all burning, little bright lights against the endless dull gray of the ash-and-stone-covered landscape.

The city was cool from the smoke covering the sun. But out here she can feel waves of heat rolling off the mountain.

Above the noise of Mount Vesuvius, Fabia hears a voice speaking close to her. "Thalia, it will be okay," the voice says. Fabia turns toward the sound. She knows that voice!

Two figures stand on the other side of the road.

"Do you know them?" Titus asks.

"I think I do," Fabia says. She takes a tentative step forward. "Penelope?"

The woman turns around, and when her eyes light on Fabia, she smiles widely. The expression is so at odds with their surroundings that Fabia is not sure how to respond.

"Fabia! You got out! I'm so glad." Penelope pauses like she expects Fabia to say something, then continues when she doesn't. "We got out of the villa in our carriage, but the wheels got trapped in all this ash and stone. We cut the horses loose and they bolted at the next earthquake. We've been walking since then."

Fabia looks at Thalia, still as expressionless as she had been that morning in the bakery, but no longer so pristine. She looks just like everybody else on the road.

"And is *this* Titus?" Penelope peers around Fabia at her brother.

Felix tugs gently on Fabia's sleeve, and she turns to him before she can answer Penelope. He's pulled the cloth back up over his face, hiding his appearance.

"I have to go," he whispers to her.

"No!" Fabia exclaims, but Felix gestures at her to be quiet.

"Listen, you and Titus have found some friends. Penelope is rich and well-connected. She can help you. But me?" He gestures to himself. "I'm a runaway. Nobody has recognized me yet, but Penelope definitely will. I need to leave. Now. This is my chance to be free."

Fabia knows he's right. Letting him leave now is the truest act of friendship she can give.

Her father had sworn never to enslave people and to help others anytime he could.

Fabia glances at Penelope, who is still talking to Titus.

"Good luck, Felix," she says softly to not draw attention to them.

"You, too." He puts his hand on her shoulder one last time before turning and taking a path off the main road.

He vanishes quickly into the gloom, becoming just another unidentifiable figure, another refugee from the destroyed city.

CHAPTER 15

"Who was that?" Penelope asks, looking at Felix curiously as he walks away.

"I don't know," Fabia jumps in before Titus can say anything. "He saw that we needed help and offered to help us. He was simply a very kind stranger."

She turns away from the city and the mountain and heads in the direction of the road.

The four of them walk through the night. At some point, the stones stop falling. Fabia recognizes the change, but she's so tired that she doesn't say anything. She's not sure how much it even matters at this point.

"Look," Titus says, nudging Fabia. He points at the sky. "Stars."

All of them pause. Fabia takes a deep breath, realizing that the air is clearer here.

Just as her anxiousness has started to fade, a sound rips through the night. Just like when the mountain first exploded that afternoon, the sound is deeper than a noise. It is more like a physical force that rushes over them, shoving their hearts back in their chests.

It's like a wave the size of the mountain is roaring over the land, but though all of them look around, no one can find a cause.

"We'd better keep moving," Penelope says.

Fabia's knees buckle under the weight of helping prop up Titus. Thalia takes a step closer to Fabia.

"I can help him," Thalia says, so quiet that Fabia can barely make out what she says.

She offers a hand to Titus, and Fabia lets her take over. It's unexpected, but Fabia is happy for any help they can get. They keep moving, away from whatever caused that horrible crushing sound.

Fabia's eyes start to droop, but she forces herself to keep going. She only has enough concentration left to focus on one step at a time.

A soft yellow light begins to wash the world, and Fabia realizes that the sun has started to rise. They've walked through the whole night without stopping.

Then, that sound again. Another giant wave, from behind them. As one, the group turns to see what it is.

The top of the mountain seems to blow off in a gigantic explosion as more smoke and ash pour into the sky. Except, unlike before, this cloud doesn't rise. It collapses, sweeping down the side of the mountain.

Even from this distance, Fabia can feel the heat of it as a choking wave.

Penelope gasps, and Fabia realizes that her villa must have been in the wave's path. It's gone now, obliterated.

The wave stops short of the city walls, and just as Fabia is about to feel relieved, it happens again. And again.

Each wave gets closer to Pompeii, closer to her home. The air is so hot that Fabia turns away, shielding her face as her companions do the same.

Finally, the heat dissipates, and the noise stops. All together, they turn to look back. Pompeii is gone.

Fabia is speechless.

The whole city has been wiped from the face of the earth, like it was never there to begin with.

Even the harbor is gone, replaced with a field of black, smoking ash. Just the tips of a few buildings stick up from the decimated landscape. It is completely unrecognizable.

She looks at Vesuvius, but the mountain has stopped smoking. The tip of it is gone, and the

mountain is now much shorter than it was before. It looks as if its insides have been scooped out and spread across the land.

"What are we going to do?" Titus asks, sadness in his voice. The mountain isn't rumbling anymore, and the air is unnaturally still.

"I think it's over," Fabia says. She lowers herself and Titus to the ground. "I think we're safe. But we have to find Mother and Father."

Titus is already shaking his head before she's even finished. "No, they're gone," he says.

"Father said he would get Mother out and meet us on the road," Fabia argues with increasing desperation.

Titus gestures to the stillness around them. Nobody has passed the four of them since the evening before, and they haven't met anybody stopped on the road. "If they'd gotten out, they'd be here now. But they're not."

"No," Fabia protests, but it's weak. She knows Titus is right, even though she doesn't want it to be true.

Even when they were at their most desperate trying to escape the city, she always thought they would get to meet back up with their parents at the end.

But now they are gone. Their home is destroyed. Fabia's whole body aches from grief. Without the promise of reuniting with her parents, she can't fathom how she could ever take another step.

"Where will we go? What will we do?" Her voice is small and pleading.

"What about your brother?" Penelope asks. She and Thalia join them on the ground, all of their shoulders drooped with exhaustion and misery. "You said he's in Rome, correct?"

Fabia nods, not taking her eyes off the remains of her city. The sight is beginning to blur with tears she's not sure how to repress.

"How would we even get there? That's miles and miles, and I don't know the way."

And, though she doesn't say this, she has no idea how she'd get Titus there. She's not sure that she could walk the whole distance, much less Titus.

And once they got to Rome, how would they even find Lucius? A million people live there. Finding one would be almost impossible.

"We can help you," Thalia volunteers. "Can't we, Mother?"

Fabia looks at her, surprised. Thalia almost never talks, and when she does, her voice is usually so quiet she's almost inaudible, like when she'd offered to help earlier.

Now, her words are clear and loud, spoken with conviction. She looks between Fabia and her mother.

"Of course," Penelope says, nodding.

Fabia nods, her throat closed with sadness. She puts an arm around Titus's shoulder, and she looks over to see him crying, too. The tears make clean tracks down his cheeks.

"We can do it," he says quietly. Fabia leans her head against his for a minute, the two of them looking out at the ruins of their home.

"Let's go," she says finally, wiping at her face with the heels of her hands.

It won't hide the tears—nothing can. At least it makes her feel a little better.

The four of them climb to their feet, weary and aching. It feels like Fabia has been walking forever, but she knows that her journey, and Titus's, is just beginning.

Discussion Questions

1. Fabia and her brother Titus had to work together to escape Pompeii. Neither one of them could have done it alone. Discuss three examples of how they helped each other. What is a time you used teamwork to get through a challenging situation?

2. Why do you think Felix decided to help Fabia and Titus? Why does Felix leave them at the end of the book?

3. What are some of the emotions Fabia feels throughout the book? How would you feel if you were in her place? What actions would you take?

4. This story takes place a very long time ago, in the year 79. What questions would you

have for Fabia about life in Pompeii? In what ways do you think Fabia's life was different from yours? In what ways do you think her life was similar?

5. How does Fabia change over the course of her story? What does she learn about herself or those around her?

6. What do you think might happen to Fabia and Titus after the story ends? Discuss what you think the next year of their lives would have looked like.

7. What were some new words you learned reading this book? How could you use those words in telling your own *Against the Odds* story?

The Truth Behind the Tale

This story is a work of fiction, but it is based on true events and real accounts of the disaster.

Sometime on or around October 24, 79 CE, Mount Vesuvius, located near the Bay of Naples in Italy, erupted.

The Romans who occupied the surrounding area had no idea that the mountain was a volcano. They also didn't have the scientific understanding of what volcanoes are in the way we do today. Many fled out of fear of the unknown, most escaping overland, and some by sea. The eruption destroyed agriculture, homes, and the cities built in the volcano's shadow. The most famous of these is Pompeii, a port city with a population between twelve and twenty thousand.

The eruption began sometime around noon, with a large plume of smoke emerging from the top of the mountain. The winds quickly moved the cloud to cover the city, and ash began to fall. A type of stone called pumice fell at a rate of about six inches per hour.

Over the course of the day, Vesuvius continued to erupt, sending ash, cinders, and hot volcanic rock high into the sky, forming a column above the mouth of the volcano. Once it cooled, in the early hours of the morning, the column collapsed, creating what's called a pyroclastic flow that moved rapidly down the mountain and into the bay. Pyroclastic flows are made of hot rock and ash mixed with volcanic gas at temperatures of more than 500 degrees Fahrenheit. Nobody in its path could survive.

This happened several times throughout the night, and by about six o'clock the next morning, the eruption had wound down. By that point, almost all of Pompeii was gone, buried under many feet of volcanic material.

The city was rediscovered a few times over the years, but true excavation of the city didn't begin until the 1700s. Work is still being done there today, and millions of people visit the archaeological site each year to walk among the ruins of the buildings. The city gives us a snapshot of Roman life at the moment of the eruption, from carbonized loaves of bread found still in bakery ovens to graffiti done by children on the walls of the buildings.

Slavery was common in Roman society. Enslaved people were often treated cruelly. Some people, like Fabia's father, did manage to buy their way out of slavery, but this option wasn't available for everyone.

Pompeii is also known for its fabulous and intricate mosaics laid throughout the city in both private and public areas. Many of them are still visible today in their original places in the ruins of Pompeii or kept safe in museums.

One of the most famous mosaics depicts a dog, which were popular pets in Roman times, the same way they are today.

Although in the story, Fabia helps her father with his work, it's unlikely that she would have been allowed to do so in real life. There's not much information remaining about the lives of Roman women and children, particularly of the working classes, but free women generally stayed in the home. Some women ran businesses or worked as hairdressers, midwives, or even doctors, but this was uncommon.

EXPLORE MORE TITLES IN THE THRILLING AGAINST THE ODDS SERIES

SAN FRANCISCO EARTHQUAKE 1906
HC 9780593962688
PB 9780593962671

Morphology focus: Common prefixes and verb suffixes

ANIMAL ATTACKS
HC 9780593962749
PB 9780593962732

Collection of three short stories
Morphology focus: Multiple suffixes

CRASHED!
HC 9780593962725
PB 9780593962718

Collection of three short stories
Morphology focus: Suffixes that mean the state or result of

Scan to visit the website for more resources!